# WHO WANTS ROCKS?

by Michael Arvaarluk Kusugak
art by Vladyana Langer Krykorka

Annick Press Ltd.
Toronto • New York • Vancouver

We acknowledge the support of the Canada Council for the Arts for our publishing program.
We also thank the Ontario Arts Council.

We acknowledge the financial support of the Government of Canada through the
Book Publishing Industry Development Program for our publishing activities.

**Cataloguing in Publication Data**

Kusugak, Michael
Who wants rocks?

ISBN 1-55037-589-X (bound)  ISBN 1-55037-588-1 (pbk.)

I. Krykorka, Vladyana. II. Title.

PS8571.U53W46  1999    jC813'.54    C99-930693-6
PZ7.K87Wh  1999

The art in this book was rendered in pen and watercolors.
The text was typeset in Bernhard Modern.

Distributed in Canada by:
Firefly Books Ltd.
3680 Victoria Park Avenue
Willowdale, ON
M2H 3K1

Published in the U.S.A. by:
Annick Press (U.S.) Ltd.
Distributed in the U.S.A. by:
Firefly Books (U.S.) Inc.
P.O. Box 1338, Ellicott Station
Buffalo, NY 14205

Printed and bound in Canada by
Friesens, Altona, Manitoba.

For Peter, my brother.
M.A.K.

To Ian, for being such a cool son.
V.L.K.

People talk about moving mountains.
Yukon Territory, in Arctic Canada, is the only place on earth
I know of where they actually do it.
This story came to me in Dawson City, Yukon.
—Michael Kusugak

Little Mountain looked about her. There were big mountains all around. Ravens flew about. Birds sang in her trees. Rabbits hopped here and there. Mountain goats climbed up and down her cliffs.

There was peace. Little Mountain was happy.

Mountains stand in magnificent splendor, showing the world their great height, their majestic silence and their impenetrable armor.

But Little Mountain was not silent. She spoke to the world around her through the breeze in her trees. "Come and live with me," she said. "I have lean times and times when my grasses and fruits are plentiful. But I have lived long and well. Come and live with me."

People came. The animals came.

Birds came. Life was good.

One day, Old Joe arrived carrying his pick and his shovel and his pan. Old Joe was a prospector. He had looked for gold all his life. He dreamed of riches, as prospectors will. He had been rewarded with gold and silver now and then, but he had not found that big strike that would make him rich, really rich.

Old Joe climbed a great mountain pass and down again. It was not so much a pass as a great climb up and down. He climbed another and down again. This is Yukon Territory in Canada's great Arctic. There are many mountains and many mountain passes.

Old Joe was hot and tired. His face and shirt were wet with sweat. Flies buzzed around his head. Mosquitoes bit his neck. No-see-'ems flew into his ears and his nose. He slapped at them, flailing his arms about.

He dipped his pan into the cool waters of a stream in the valley below Little Mountain. He moved the pan in a circular motion, making the water swirl around and around. The sand flowed out of the pan with the swirling water. He dipped his pan back into the stream, swatted more flies and continued making the water move around and around, letting the sand flow out of the pan with the water. At the bottom of the pan was shiny yellow sand. It glistened in the sun. He looked closely at it, moving it around with his fingertips.

"Gold!" he yelled at the top of his lungs, jumping up and down and dancing a jig on the spot.

Soon other prospectors came from the South, long lines
of prospectors who climbed the steep mountain passes
and down again, carrying all their prospecting and mining
equipment with them.

"Gold!" they yelled, and were heard all over the world.

Before long the streams were full of prospectors
and miners with their pans and sluices, looking
for the precious gold. They staked
every bit of land.

Old Joe saw the miners digging all around him. "Why did I yell 'Gold!' so loud?" he asked himself. "I have to stop doing that. Now they have all the gold and I have none."

He climbed a mountain just to the north of Little Mountain. He began to dig with his pick and shovel. He found a gold nugget. He looked at it, amazed at how big it was. Just at that moment a mosquito flew into his ear. He slapped at it, *smack!* He heard a ringing in his ear that made him dizzy.

He yelled "Gold!", twice as loud as before. He could not stop himself; the word just came out. He wasn't thinking very well with all the bugs that were bothering him.

Soon the other prospectors and miners were digging all over North Mountain. They got richer and richer, except for Old Joe. "I just have to stop yelling 'Gold!' so loud," he said to himself.

Northern Mountain got smaller and smaller, until there was no more mountain. All that was left of him was rubble.

"Poor North Mountain," thought Little Mountain. North Mountain would never again have birds flying about him. He would never again have animals feeding on his grasses. Streams would never flow from his sides. People would never camp on his slopes.

"Poor North Mountain," thought Little Mountain again, and her streams flowed even more.

The prospectors and miners climbed another mountain.

"Gold!" they yelled.

Before long, that mountain too was gone. And poor Little Mountain was sadder still. Mountains were falling all around her, turning to rubble, and there was nothing she could do about it.

Old Joe climbed Little Mountain. He began to dig into her side. Little Mountain shuddered. Old Joe dug and dug. But all he found were rocks. Rocks, rocks and more rocks.

He slapped a mosquito in his other ear and was dizzy again for a moment. He had a thought. "Every time I yell 'Gold!' they all come following me. Let's see what they think of rocks. If I am not going to get rich, I might as well have some fun. He laughed and slapped his forehead, *smack!*

"Rocks!" he yelled, really loud.

There was a short silence while the people down below thought about what Old Joe had said. Then someone called back from down below: "Rocks? Who wants rocks!"

All the other prospectors and miners yelled, "Rocks? Who wants rocks!!" like an echo from the mountains all around.

Old Joe laughed and climbed another side of Little Mountain.

"Rocks!" he yelled again.

All the people down below yelled back, "Rocks? Who wants rocks!"

Old Joe was having a good time. He climbed a big mountain just to the east of Little Mountain. He began to dig.

"Rocks!" he thought, with a smile on his wrinkled, suntanned face. He said nothing. He would never find gold again, he thought. He had looked for gold all his life. He had found gold, but he had not become rich. Why was it, when he found gold, other prospectors and miners got rich and he did not? He was disheartened.

He sat down. A breeze blew in his face, keeping the bugs away. The sun was low to the west. He looked at Little Mountain. Ravens flew around her. Caribou grazed on her lush grasses. Birds sang in her trees. Rabbits drank from her cool streams. People camped on her slopes. Mountain goats climbed up and down her cliffs. And moose ate from the marshes all around her.

"This is the most beautiful sight I have ever seen," he said. "And if it wasn't for rocks, we would have torn it all down."

He sat there for a long time enjoying the scene, the
fresh, fresh air, the smell of the trees and the sounds of
nature all around him. Tears came to his eyes.

"These are the riches I have been looking for all my
life," he said. "Thank god for rocks."

"Thank god for rocks," Little Mountain said. Deep
inside her, way down beneath all the rocks, was the shiniest
heart anyone has ever seen.

Big Mountain said, "Thank god for rocks." He too had
a big heart of gold hidden way down beneath the rocks.

Old Joe built a cabin on Big Mountain.
He could see Little Mountain from his
front door. He still lived by prospecting
and mining, though he did not
make much money.

Old Joe was happy. No more mountains turned to rubble because of him.

He told stories about Little Mountain. He wrote poems about her. And every day Old Joe looked at her and said to himself, "Who wants rocks? I do. Thank god for rocks."

Taima